I0534025

Poetry by AC Benus

Hymenaios, or The Marriage of the God of Marriage
A Classical style myth in 2,600 lines of Blank Verse
ebook: ISBN 9781953389091; paperback: ISBN 9781953389084

Summer 2020 – Hell in a Handbasket
A contender for the Pulitzer Prize in poetry, 2021, this collection grapples with the year of pandemic, racial justice and environmental crisis
ebook: ISBN 9781953389015; paperback: ISBN 9781953389008

The Thousandth Regiment
A Translation of and Commentary on Hans Ehrenbaum-Degele's War Poems "Das tausendste Regiment"
ebook: ISBN 1657220583; paperback: ISBN 9781657220584

A Man in a Room and other poems
Poems written when AC Benus was 21 years old
ebook: ISBN 97817345103; paperback: ISBN 978173456107

The Easiest Thing in the World
And other poems: marking the third anniversary of the Pulse Nightclub attack
ebook: ISBN 9781734561029; paperback: ISBN 9781734561036

Rima Fragmenta, or Fragments of a Rift
Fifty Sonnet for Kevin
ebook: ISBN 9781734561005; paperback: ISBN 9781734561012

First Love: Poems for Ross
For everyone's first love, both bitter and sweet
ebook: ISBN 9781734561081; paperback: ISBN 9781734561098

AC Benus

Love Looked at Me and Laughed

– and other poems for Brian –

an AC Benus Impression
San Francisco

Grateful acknowledgement is here offered
for the support and encouragement
I've received on the literary site
www.gayauthors.org.

ISBN 978-1-953389-23-7 (ebook)
ISBN 978-1-953389-22-0 (paperback)
ISBN 978-1-953389-24-4 (hardback)

LOVE LOOKED AT ME AND LAUGHED:
AND OTHER POEMS FOR BRIAN.
Copyright © 2022 by AC Benus.
All rights reserved.
No part of this book may be used or reproduced in any manner
whatsoever without written permission, except in the case of
brief quotations embodied in critical articles and reviews.

Cover photo:
Christine Sponchia / Pixabay.com

Feather vignette:
Yuri B / Pixabay.com

Library of Congress Control Number: 2022904914

Love
Looked
at Me and
Laughed

Poem No. 1

first poem

      If I say it now,
   and say it for seventy years more,
will one day you truly believe . . . ? [1]

---

[1] Brian was my first boyfriend; my first reciprocated love

Poem No. 2

Prelude:

What need I do
what need I say
to prove this is real

What words to write
what thoughts to speak
to make you believe

For the night was fragile
and in the end, the sun prevailed
for it was much too soon to end
what things of wonder we began

So

What need I be
what words to pen
to prove this is real

When words too frail
to hold what has gone
trust me not to fail
I'll keep through the dawn

What need I do
what need I say
to prove this is real

What words to write
what thoughts to speak
to make you believe

For the night was fragile
and in the end, the sun prevailed
for it was much too soon to end
what things of wonder we began

Poem:

Seven o'clock, Eight o'clock,
    Nine o'clock, ten,
Why doesn't it ring, with news of him.

Eleven o'clock, Noon, one and two,
    What madness not to be with you.

Three till five, and five till Nine,
    Is there no relief, no peace of mind.

From ten till seven,
    All hope is gone;
Oh, God, please let this scenario be wrong.

No answer yet has come,
    Sweet sorrow, for what was begun.

Postlude:

Is love just a trick
that can be pulled from the air

like a furry white rabbit
from a hat that doesn't play fair.

From nowhere can it appear
with no warning or rhyme
like an actor from backstage
who knows not his lines.

No, love is surrender
and suddenly it's free
no weapons were needed
only the you and the me.

Love is no trick
that's certain enough
for all of its kindness
it's frightening stuff.

Poem No. 3

You've found a place in me,
I didn't know was there.
Where light dances with me,
and all else seems fair.

A place I've never known,
nearer to each than his own.
What a surprise to discover,
that life is about Me.

You've found the place in me,
where I never want to be alone.
Come dance with me,
and be my own.

Poem No. 4

Prelude:

No act, no game
    none I swear
what I feel now
    is in no way fair

You trust me not
    you doubt my heart
no pain can be greater
    than to never have that

Stop it, don't you know
    with every word, with every look
the feeling only grows
    and deeper into the Misery you send me

It's no act, no game
    what fool would practice
self-mutilation
    for the thought of love

Poem:

How can I say it now
that it seems not untrue
those simple words
that are said too much to be true

I love you in simple truth
no torture could be as sweet
those simple words
that are too much to be true

   Postlude:

Don't fear me,
    my Love,
    and fear not my love

I didn't live
    before you
    but hold you dearer than my life

      II.
Let go of the fear
and open your eyes
I am what you see
I am what you want

Poem No. 5

May I find the happiness of a
Million years condensed to the thought
Of you

A thousand lifetimes can never know
The bliss I've found within your glow
How sweet the chance to dream of you
How sad the day I cannot touch you

Dare I summon your image
Dare I ask this torture to never end
And dare I thank the stars
From which you were sent

For I find the joy of a million years
Condensed to the thought and moment
Of you

Poem No. 6

Prelude:

Life's a game
that none will win
a fact that
no longer matters to me.
Not the same
did we begin
this thing which
words will no longer give me.

Poem:

Shall I say it loud; shall I say it soft
Shall I sing it; shall I shout it
    Which way do you want to hear it?

Poem No. 7

I want to be
what I see reflected
    in your eyes.

Poem No. 8

   Prelude:

I love you as the
    Morning loves the Night
    as Earth loves the Rain
    as Birds love their Flight

I want my words
to be like daggers through your heart
I want each one
to kill the person you once were
to be replaced
with the one who only loves me more

For I love you as the
   Seaside loves the Sea
   as Snow loves the Cold;
   like joining Lovers at parting
   Like Hope begging to Dream

I love you as all of these
   love me.

   Poem:

There in your dulcet kiss
I search for the Never
hoping I do not miss
your taste of Forever

Poem No. 9

Sweet Murderer of my heart
    Kind kidnapper of my senses
    My only wish is that you never return
    That which you took.

Poem No. 10

  Prelude:

More beautiful than the gold of old
Your image haunts me now
Of words yet to be told –
My only quest is how.

  Poem:

Do you know why,
Have the reason to explain,
How in your embrace I die
And yet the pleasure remains?
Reasons, I find them not at all;
The source I find in my arms

Like the memory of a primal call –
Too close to recognize the alarm.
Oh, the wonder
There between our touch;
A new kind of hunger,
One I cannot get too much.
    Do you know why I love you? –
        in words I know not either;
    I thank the Fates I found you,
        and pray you're a believer.

    Postlude:

Snow and ice are outside
but warm am I with your thought.

Poem No. 11

I lie in bed within the night
and beseech her answer –
my plea ascends up to her might

Fastidious darkness finds me
    within my empty bed
catches, moves, feels, and then she sees
    the thoughts I fill her head
those questions of questing intrigue –
    her gentle ear I bend –
on how it can be
    I hold only this pen

Has love left me
and where did she send
all the energy of his heart?

Poem No. 12

To be free of this freedom
    where two people
    together drown
    in their loneliness

I am just bracing myself
    for the torment
    that will follow
    from your next descent

I have no more freedom
    than I want to have
    and dream
    in the pleasure of your smile

Poem No. 13

Prelude:

Impotent, powerless love,
    unable to control even the least.

Ineffectual to change you or the world,
    I can't even make you believe me.

I am no comfort to your every solace,
    I am no relief to your every pain.

Impotent, powerless am I
    to affect your sight of me.

And yet, this love for you
    only burns the brighter;
every moment with you
    fuels the passion lighter.

I love you, that I know,
    and there's nothing you can do
to make it any less so –
    there's nowhere for me to go.

Through the pain of it all,
    through misunderstanding's call,
however often you fall
    I'll be constant through it all.

For I love you;
    my sweet surrender to the fact
has left me with nothing to prove,
    yet paralyzed to act.

  Poem:

There is a love few of us know.
It springs upon you suddenly,
And when the time must come to let it go,
It can hit you horribly.
When you've looked for it for so long,
And given up hope of finding,
Then you will tumble over it headlong,
And not remember ever standing.
There is a love few of you know.
It leaves you staggered in pain,
Begging for it to simply go,
But terrified it won't remain.

My love for you is my life;
Every breath only heightens it.

From now to the end of my fight,
I must rejoice having known it.

Poem No. 14

Poem:

What madness is this thing called love
    Here idolatry passes for normal
    Here's where casual seems far too casual
Where two different hands fit into a glove

Frustration faces the everyday
    with a face like none other I know
    A wall I want to melt with my every breath
with a face like none other I've known

Waster of the greatest thing we have
    Here exasperation finds your face
    Here you simply don't see the nature of space
Waster of Time. I lament the loss of every
    minute we have failed to be.

Postlude:

    It's your delusions that I am fighting
    a battle I fear I shall not win.

Poem No. 15

I'm some kind of tormentor
one you'd simply rather
have go away.

You're always thinking
about my leaving you –
aren't you?

Poem No. 16

Roses in puddles of milk
Honey on whole wheat bread
I too know the longing
of Love's madness.

Poem No. 17

There is a selfishness that only siblings can breed,
From the stranglehold of sharing they long to be free.
Self-protection for the heart,
Mere corrections for the mind.
Prying mentors from the start,
Are aggravations left behind.

Poem No. 18

When in the chronicle of wasted time
the chapter is turned to thoughts of you
I must shut the volume closed again
not finding a single entry there.

No second spent with you
was ever one of waste.

Poem No. 19

Sweet the night that brings you back to me
relieved of the everyday sorrows

Poem No. 20

To find you there
in my first waking thought
no longer does grip me
without surprise

How many ways can I say it:
night and day, before and after.
How to say it, so you will know
I love you now, as I loved you then

To find you there
the last before I sleep
no longer worries me.
I hope you've come to the same

Poem No. 21

Love is surrender, and that you could never do.
No pain could be greater.
To come to a fact, and find where
you hoped it wouldn't be

Poem No. 22

No armies of the world,
now, or all the ones passed,
possessed power to conquer
the task I have been given

Poem No. 23

Prelude:

How many times did he do the dishes?
    I know not
His motives for doing them with such fervor?
    I know not

We ask questions to discover what we don't know.
Why we ask them, do any of us know?

There are so many solutions, more than questions
    I know not
My own motives for asking them with such fervor?
    I know not

Poem:

    State enough solutions
        and one day you'll find the right question.

    Postlude:

Dare we displace the mysteries that are?
    Turn the rock of the question,
and be stung by the scorpion of truth?

Life is too short to ask it all,
    forever too narrow to know it all,
death only a hiccup in the quest.

What answers do I need to live?
    Only that it's my chance to give
more questions to those yet to live.

Poem No. 24

I'm not who I was
    the fact is clear
But is the who I want to be
    anymore near

My words, my hurts
into your heart are sent
there the power of reserves
knocks down your best defense
it is a victory I do not want
a joy that won't

Poem No. 25

The future stretches ahead of me
    in a vast array,
Speaking of the wonder of a million things
    there are yet to say.

Poem No. 26

Living is wondering why you have life;
Contentment is knowing you have life to live. [2]

---

[2] Written on the day I said goodbye to Brian before moving to Japan

Poem No. 27

Optimism wanes, reality finds
    I am alone
Help disdains, sorrow binds
    I am alone
Memory pains, worry reminds
    I am alone.

Poem No. 28

Love looked at me and laughed,
For it saw how blind I was to that;
His heart hooked into me but half.

Love looked at me and laughed,
All the time it saw and knew,
His heart hooked in me but half.

Love looked at me and laughed,
All the time it saw and knew,
His heart hooked in me but half;
That was plain to all, but nothing new.
Love looked at me and laughed.

Poem No. 29

Prelude:

We filled the 7-Eleven
    with energy.
The lady attendant
    felt it, but did not understand.
She stood there, and sensed it all around her,
    wondered why she suddenly felt different,
looked and found it in every corner,
    listened and heard it in every sound.
The little 7-Eleven glowed,
    but could not contain it.
The lady attendant felt, but,
    could not understand it.

Poem:

What power could be greater,
what force could break through,
two hearts together
in the hour when love is new.
No strength has been its equal,
no single heart its rival,
two minds their sequel,
in the hour of love's arrival.
Every goal has its dreams,
that everyone wants true,
no matter how it seems;
whatever action it might do.
    All the 7-Elevens in the world,
        could not contain
    What the lady attendant
        could not explain.

Poem No. 30

My worth is gilded with grime,
Leaving nothing to me
Except inexpressible longing.

Poem No. 31

There must be no retreat from the fact.
I must return every look for the value it was given,
with no fear that it was ever less or more.
I must force my sun to rise, for they to see,
the 'they' for whom my light will have its meaning.

Poem No. 32

Must I stay in this mask of my own making,
Pretending the world knows not the difference
Between who I am and the possibilities forsaken,
Showing only mistaken deliverance?
And so, as the option wanes,
and I for want of better,
look at what little remains,
by turning it into a burden.
Any longer need I the mask indeed,
But for the weight of years of feared accusing.

Poem No. 33

My brand of sorrow
is their livelihood;
their brand of sadness
is my muse.

A Poem about the Psychiatric Profession

Poem No. 34

What can all the fierce greenness of spring
possibly mean to a heart without love.

    The emptiness there
    cannot be filled by
    the entire intake of the eyes.

I cannot see the spring for its worth;
cannot fill my heart empty of your love.

Poem No. 35

  Look at me sitting there
the master of nothing
  Mastering the role of
a victim to none but me
  Watching in horror
as the night feeds upon
  what little stock I've stored.

Poem No. 36

Last night the moon spoke your name to me,
And it was all I could do to bear it.
In her rising light she said,
"Let the morning be for song;
Let the night revolve in tears
For the lost realm of your love."

> *Why did I love you for the emptiness it brought;*
> *That bore down on a heart too young to know*
> *The price of torment your peace required?*

My average words and my average voice
Climbed up to her in her all-knowing splendor.
"Shall I ever sing of joy in the night . . . "
Her answer was, "Let the sorrow be your song."
And it was all I could to do bear it,
For I knew it must be so

> *The price of torment your peace required?*
> *It bore down on a heart too young to know,*
> *So why did I love the emptiness it brought.*

Poem No. 37

In your appearance
I wonder why I wonder
If you be the reason
    Of my pain

Poem No. 38

What be the nature of this desire
that courses through my veins
that rips apart my brains
whichever saps my power

Ever am I drawn near to you
for the sweet sorrow in your smiles
playing witness to your other wiles
and my torment gone through . . .

But what is the quality of the want
that filters you into my head
with longings impossibly said
with desire of only the want . . .

Poem No. 39

If while I slept the while away
    a Muse came and stole my tongue someday –
crept between open curtains did,
    slithered round my rug and in bed slid
with passionate thought of a lurid kiss,
    low-seducing lips uncoiling a hiss –
my sleeping tongue aroused by hers
    might abandon me when her favor lures.

        When the first light of night
        broke through my window
        and fell upon my floor,
        it found me there
        with pen in hand,
        and you in heart.

And in that light
I faded near away
to another shady sight
of a place so far afield,
time seemed its equal,
and I but cast adrift.

On another floor was I –
at a different light did look –
through the windowpane
shone the full face of torment
caused then as now
by a wilding moon.

Underneath me was
a floor of a different kind,
support from other regions
which vanish only when
names get tagged to them;
when hopes from them are craved.

Rang true the voice
asking me what I want;
sincere the look
that said I didn't know;
for the spirit of the desire
is yet beyond me now.

Calm were the eyes
which asked me for my hand;

quaking was the heart
that handed it there,

softly delivered
unto your waiting touch.

Adrift the waves of night
midway 'tween dream and world –
as the sleepy specter
ever crept her gain –
I never had
the fear I fight with now.

The thought to worry,
though drowsy were my eyes
and inactive were my limbs,
never before on a countless level
could I make claim
to ever be more awake.

So how can I,
at once adrift in two lights,
perceive which is true:
the hand that touched me there
with the greatest wonder known,
or the drifting sight upon my eyes?

I loved you then
as I love you now;
sweet wonder that it can live
astride the crater of time
in hopeless lapse of another
chance for what never was.

And if while I slept the while someday,
    a Muse came to steal my tongue away,
she would turn a very startled head
    at the odd things her new tongue said,
and woe behold that muse of mine,
    for that wagging thing by rights is thine;
it can speak of no other heart but yours,
    and with words alone your memory endures.

Poem No. 40

The eternal struggle:
to deal with
the loss that never incurred.

Poem No. 41

Prelude:

To subdue on paper, a grant of words.
To tempt them here, and nail in ink
A seduction of formless sighs,
In tender strokes of terror's guise.
With fingers so-stained, to it I'll sink;
The open call of my lover, to grant me words.

Poem:

Beauty take me where the shoulders join,
in the soft valley where one folds into the other
caress me there as I'd never before met
with gentle hand set upon vicious fingers

Beauty subdue me where lobe finds jaw,
where one curve melts to the face's strength
kiss me there with lips of stony red
and the breath of fire's own passion

Find a place for me beneath cotton and silk,
where all that moves, is Want's embody
consume me there to the length of my desire
where power becomes form; and form, its grace

On Eighth and Forty-Eighth you'll find
three building entries with raised stoops,

of old melting sandstone columns
and rapidly fading red paint.
      The addresses' segregation
      is measured by spans of plywood
      alive with handbills in decay,
      and gravity taking its due.

And in a time, some years ago,
I would walk my way slowly past
and consider how I felt there
was something almost wrong right here.
      For its dirt and grime can't make
      cityscapes match their perfect goals
      when it shakes up the steppers-by
      with notions of the not yet done.

Not Beauty, for surely I thought,
she would be nowhere near to this
fairly forlorn, forsaken place;
here was no one but Her rival.
      But all those years I walked ago,
      those stones like a flint became struck,
      and in many ways of it now,
      the sparks of that fire still glow.

In the night and on the sidewalk,
Past two stoops and their yawning voids,
I to the dirty third one came
To see in the dark lurked a light.
      Some bright angel was for the rent
      Wearing a perfect set of white –
      But more than his jeans and his shirt,
      His looks spoke of his business role.

He told me, yes, he understood;
told me *he'd* be able to care;
told me all I wanted to hear,
and could say it without the words.
    Approaching, he came down three steps
    and stood like a Grace for me there
    with promise of much more than that
    and the sad thought I might accept.

Out of the rectangle of night
his persona molded to me;
to match die-cast to my desire,
he poured himself entirely.

    He had the same eyes as Beauty
    but their hue was nothing lovely,
    and I found in their knowing glow
    I could want for nothing if chose.
        But I'd choose the endless knowing
        of the speechless sorrow in him.

From out a corner of the night
I asked him in my lonely quest
if he could tell which half of me
I'd discovered amiss in him.
    He said he did not have a clue
    but wondered if that could matter,
    for see, did he not there command
    the looks of a sweet businessman?

So, for an end of this, I'll say –
here, now, I feel alive with words,

but what I wanted then from him
sticks with me and makes me ask:
    Who can breathe life in me of form?
    From which dark corner of the night
    might I find the answers I seek;
    from whom might I take the breath of life?

    Yet I'd choose the endless knowing
    of the speechless sorrow in him.

Beauty take me where the shoulders meet,
where under covers, let my hands tease
the crashing planes of muscled forms
with fingertips on easy glide
Let my lips caress Beauty's ear,
and fill it with my wordless sighs –
of Want in the costumes of air –
not the disguise of speechless worth

Allow me to throw my arms up,
to kiss the nape from lobes downwards,
and know everything I encountered
was put there by Beauty to be found

  Postlude:

Can, on the face of this, I lure;
Here on paper draw out for you
The sweet breath of the morn?

When all the pillars cannot endure –
when every sound I utter through –
Collapses onto your feet of scorn?

My lungs cannot secure –
Here exhale for you –
How I was met by that morn.

Poem No. 42

Poem:

In lovely sorrow I sink again,
to the depths of a familiar deep,
as fingers in aging glove descend,
to borrow themselves a state complete.
Around my decline the white shirts land,
in lines as pure as bleach can render,
while I ask if any understand,
the soundless graft of my encover.
Here where I stand is murky and loud,
with other laughter swirling the air,

as we the ever-damned of the crowd,
must seek our diversion into a pair.
For he who plummets to this depth of mine,
Sorrow save him from the joy he'll find.

Postlude:

Oh, to have heart and voice the same;
Skill enough to bleed talent un-lame.

Poem No. 43

To view a sorrow as a fact,
    is a precarious point to make;
It negates room to enact
    a retreat from its mistake.

Poem No. 44

I turn the pages,
and admire the loves long dead.
I put on their eyes to admire
the loves they longed.

And with every word
I hear them speak of you,
and give form in my wont
of expression.

Poem No. 45

I'm sorry I cannot
                tame it
And ever here
                retain it

Poem No. 46

The three of me
were quite surprised to see
the shock you there received,
for I am what I seem.
What did it mean
that look you gave
what turmoil did it say
what reaction grave.
For men are of parts three
Mind, Dick and heart . . .
and though I am what I seem
I have much more of me between.
Do you love me . . .
my heart strikes a *coup d'état*
and topples my head to feet
and all are quite surprised to see
the possible reason it could be.
If my love loves me
then all the wonders we shall see
if my love in love be
then great in value are we three.

Poem No. 47

" . . . amongst the books where much was read,
I pressed the leaves of a love long dead . . . "
                                    Wordsworth

Around a love long dead,
    I fold the leaves anew;
Ache through them what was said,
    Spoken in wont of you.

For the lack, autumn's never done,
    Stealing the shade of warmer fires,
Bearing centuries' comparison;
    Reading in them their own desires.

Such ashes always spring to mind
    The passions they were consumed with;
And in them can I ever find
    The madness compelling to myth.

But as these words languish in spite,
    Each one in turn has come to learn,
They but live to take my love's height,
    And never mind the pain of spurn.

Around a love long dead,
   Thoughts laid here bare and bleak,
Ache through what can't be said
   When ink alone must speak.

Poem No. 48
– several years later –

Brian

The same old problem,
The same old crisis
Where one word promises
To bloom into another;
Where one idea but poses
All the problems that
Neither poetry, nor every power
Of action incarnate
Can keep from sliding
Into old familiar excesses;
That love is nothing but
One idea promising to pull me
Deep down into another,
Old problem.

~

www.ingramcontent.com/pod-product-compliance
Lightning Source LLC
Chambersburg PA
CBHW031902170626
46807CB00004B/1863